Marks and Spencer p.l.c.
Baker Street, London, England
1428/3013

SBN 361 04927 7
Text and artwork copyright © 1980 Purnell Publishers Limited
Mrs Hedgehog character copyright © 1979 Marks and Spencer p.l.c.
Published September 1980 by Purnell Books,
Paulton, (Bristol) and London
Made and printed in Great Britain by Purnell and Sons (Book Production) Limited,
Paulton (Bristol) and London

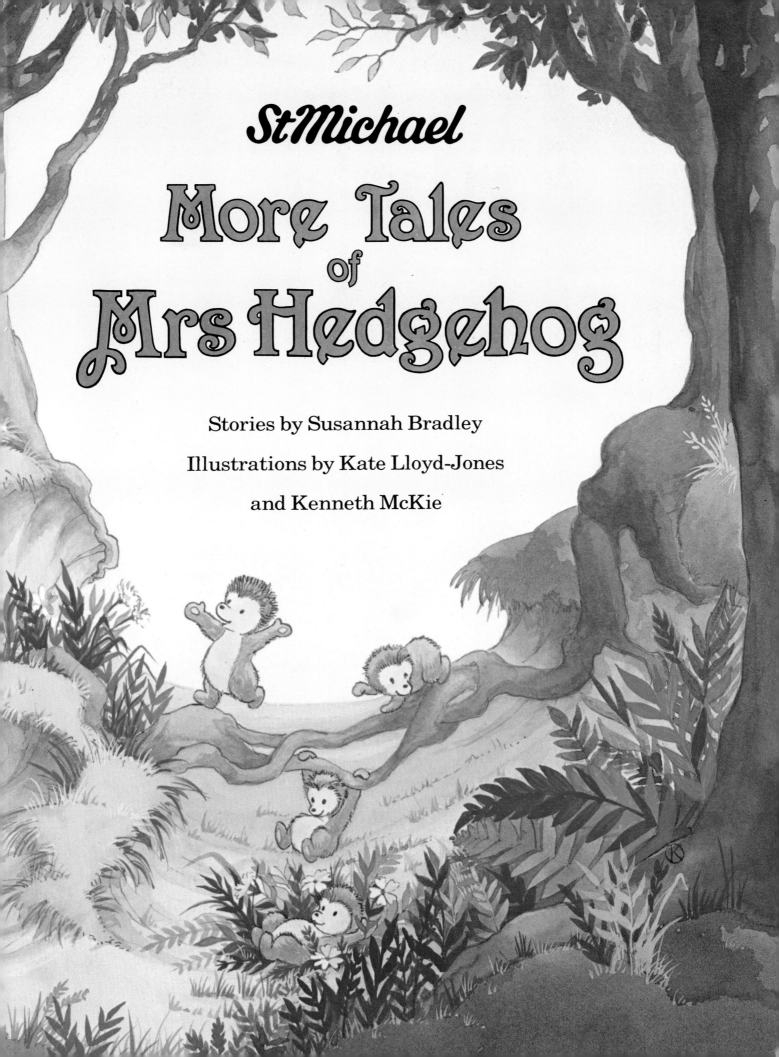

St Michael

More Tales of Mrs Hedgehog

Stories by Susannah Bradley

Illustrations by Kate Lloyd-Jones

and Kenneth McKie

Henrietta's Garden

Henrietta Hedgehog woke very early one morning to find that the sun was shining brightly through the window.

"Thank you for waking me up, sun!" she said, sitting up and rubbing her eyes. "Now I can get all my housework done before it is time to give my babies their breakfast!"

It is much easier to work at household chores while the sun is shining, and Henrietta soon had a line of washing blowing outside in the warm spring breeze. By the time the five baby hedgehogs came into the kitchen for breakfast, Henrietta had cleaned the house so that everything was sparkling.

"The washing is ready for ironing already," said Henrietta to herself, as she took the dry clothes from the line and waved to her babies as they disappeared down the woodland path to school. "It won't take me long to iron this."

The heat from the iron made Henrietta very hot indeed. "Phew!" she said out loud, as she stacked the pile of ironing in the linen cupboard. "I must go outside for a breath of air!"

Outside the burrow the sun's beams splashed across the green grass and danced overhead among the leafy branches. High up in the sky the birds were singing joyfully, and Henrietta could hear Charlie Crow telling his wife to be careful that the little ones did not fall out of the nest.

Henrietta sat down on a tree root and thought how lucky
she was to have such a nice house on ground level where
nobody could fall out of anything. She sat there for some time,
enjoying the sunshine, but soon the tree root began to feel
very uncomfortable and she had to stand up again.

"Now if I had a nice garden," thought Henrietta, "I could sit
out here in comfort and relax in the sunshine."

The more she thought about it, the more she decided that it was a good idea to plan a garden. It would be so nice to have a lawn, with flowers round the edge, where the children could play. They could have tea on it in the summer! Henrietta got more and more excited at the idea.

She fetched her purse from the kitchen and set off at once through the wood to Amanda Mole's shop.

"Good morning, Amanda!" she said. "Isn't it a lovely day?"

"It's too sunny for me, I'm afraid," said Amanda. "We moles prefer dark places, you know. We can't see a thing in all that bright sunlight, so we usually stay inside."

Because her eyes had become accustomed to the sunshine outside, Henrietta could not see a thing in Amanda's dark shop, and she said so.

"That doesn't matter," said Amanda. "I can see quite clearly in the dim light in here. You just tell me what you want and I'll get it down from the shelves for you."

"I want a trowel, please," said Henrietta. "For digging a garden. I'm going to have a lawn, and flowers, so that I can sunbathe in my very own spot."

There was a gasp and a squeak of delight from the doorway and Henrietta turned round to find that Rosemary and Amelia Rabbit had just come into the shop.

"How lovely, my dear!" said Rosemary. "Can we help?"

"Oh, I'm sure you can," said Henrietta. "Thank you very much for offering."

"I know what we can do!" said Amelia, nervously. "We could nibble the grass all nice and short for the lawn – if you'd like that."

"Oh, I would like that very much!" said Henrietta.

The three animals spent a lovely day digging and nibbling for all they were worth. Everyone who passed by asked what they were doing and was very interested to hear about the garden. They all thought it was a splendid idea.

The rabbits said they did not want any lunch, thank you, because they had eaten a lot of grass and were full up, so Henrietta brought them two glasses of mayflower cordial instead.

"Delicious!" said Amelia.

"Did you make it yourself?" said Rosemary. "I don't know where you find the time with all those babies to look after."

By mid-afternoon the lawn was finished, and Henrietta had dug all round the edge for a flower border.

"It looks very nice," said Rosemary.

"Now you will have to find some plants for it," said Amelia.

Just then, Alfie Fieldmouse and his wife came round the
bend in the path, dragging a trolley behind them.

"We've brought you some poppy seeds from the cornfield," said Alfie.

"So you can grow bright red poppies," said Mrs Fieldmouse with a smile.

"How kind of you!" exclaimed Henrietta. "Where is my rake? I shall sow them in my border at once!"

Soon, all the woodland creatures had arrived to see how the Henrietta's gardening day had gone. Even Wise Owl came and brought Henrietta a deckchair which he had found in his spare room.

"You might as well have it," he said. "I've never used it, because I don't like sitting in the sunshine."

Nobody noticed that Pippin was very quiet. He listened to all his friends chattering away and felt very sad inside, for he had no present to bring for the garden. As he looked at the flower border, where Henrietta was now sowing Alfie's seeds, he had an idea. Quietly, so that nobody saw him go, he crept away from Henrietta's busy garden.

When he returned, Henrietta was waving goodbye to her visitors and was telling the baby hedgehogs, who had just come in from school, to wash their hands before tea.

"Why, Pippin!" she said. "Where did you disappear to?"

"I've brought you some more flower seeds, Henrietta," said Pippin, proudly. "There's a funny smell about them, but don't mind that. It's only because they've been in a shed belonging to some humans."

Henrietta gasped.

"Pippin! You didn't go on to human land to get these for me, did you? How brave of you!"

Pippin smiled and felt very proud.

"It was nothing, Henrietta," he replied. "Let me help you to plant them in your new garden."

Henrietta tended her garden with great care during the following weeks. It was very exciting to see the shoots of the seeds she had sown appearing through the soil. Rosemary and Amelia called often to trim the grass, and Charlie Crow said it was the best spot in Greenglades Wood for catching worms.

"That is because I water my plants a lot to make them grow," said Henrietta. "Worms like wet soil."

One morning, when Henrietta went out to water her garden, she found that she had to lift her arm very high to sprinkle the watering can over the top of the plants. A few days later, some of the plants had grown way over her head!

"It's not your poppies, Alfie," Henrietta said to the fieldmouse when he called to see them. "They are just the right size. But some of the ones that Pippin brought must be trees!"

"Let's have a look at the packets," suggested Alfie.

Henrietta fetched them and they looked at the pictures of bright yellow flowers, small pink ones, and white and yellow daisies.

"They look all right," said Alfie. "I shouldn't worry, Henrietta."

Henrietta couldn't help worrying. As she sat on her lawn in the deckchair the plants towered over her like trees. What were they? Would they ever stop growing, she wondered?

Then one morning Henrietta looked up to see that huge flowerheads had bloomed on the top of each plant. They looked magnificent with their round sunny faces and yellow petals. The woodland folk came from far and wide to see them.

"Why, they're sunflowers!" cried the blue tits.

"They're beautiful!" said Henrietta, happily.

It didn't matter that they blocked a lot of the light from the garden. It didn't matter, either, that all the people who had come to see them had trampled all over her garden.

Nobody would ever forget Pippin's sunflowers, and nobody ever did – least of all the birds who, when the flowers finally faded, took all the seeds back to their nests for food throughout the cold winter.

Wise Owl's Dream Comes True

Henrietta Hedgehog's babies were playing tag on their way home from school one afternoon when Hilary, the smallest of the five of them, suddenly cried out in dismay.

"Whatever is the matter with you?" asked the other little hedgehogs. "Have you hurt yourself?"

"No," wailed Hilary, sitting down on a log beside the woodland path. "But I've dropped the letter that Mr Fox gave us to take home to mother!"

"You silly thing!" said Henry, who was the biggest and brightest of them all. "I told you you should have let me carry it. Well, we'd better start looking for it."

They searched and searched, but dusk was falling and they kept tripping over each other because they were not looking where they were going. Everyone was getting cross with everyone else, which often happens when people are worried, when along swooped Wise Owl. He dived down and landed next to Horace, who gave a squeak of fright and fell over.

"Beg your pardon, young fellow," said Wise Owl. "It's a bit late for you to be out, isn't it? I thought you were a shrew."

Horace explained that they had lost Mr Fox's letter and were trying to find it before they went home.

"That must be what I saw further up the path just now. I

thought it was a square stoat," exclaimed Wise Owl, "but it
was only a bit of paper. I'll go back and fetch it for you."

He flew away, and was soon back with the letter in his beak.

"Must be a jolly important sort of letter, I expect?" he said, after Henry had put it in his satchel.

"It is," said Henry. "It's from our headmaster, Mr Fox, to our mother." Wise Owl gave a deep sigh.

"Headmaster, eh? It must be nice to be a headmaster. I might have been one myself only I have to sleep in the mornings because I'm out hunting all night."

The baby hedgehogs looked at each other and said that they must be getting along. Wise Owl did not seem to hear them.

"Desks," he said, looking far away into space. "Chalk, for writing on blackboards. Books, and playtime, and everyone listening to me."

"He's daydreaming again," said Horace.

"I know," said Henry. "I think we had better go."

They reached Amanda Mole's shop just as Henrietta was putting her head round the door to ask if Amanda had seen her babies.

"Why, here they are now!" said Amanda. "Do come in, all of you. I've got some exciting news."

Henrietta, who had been about to scold the babies for being late, was too interested in what the news could be to say anything after all, so the whole family went inside and waited for Amanda to tell them all about it.

"It's Ringo Fox," said Amanda. "He's going on a fizzy something or other."

"A what?" asked Henrietta.

"Sort of lessons," said Amanda, opening a jar of Crunchy Beetle Snaps and giving one to each of the baby hedgehogs. "Learning to run faster, with the deer in Old Stag Park. He'll be away for two weeks, and he told me all about it when he came in to cancel his newspapers."

"But what about school?" exclaimed Henrietta.

Silently, because his mouth was full of Beetle Snap, Henry handed her Mr Fox's letter.

"The school will be closed while he's away!" said Henrietta, when she had read it. "It's a physical training course he's going on, to get fit before the hunting season starts again."

"I knew it was something fizzy," said Amanda. "Dear me, how inconvenient for all the mothers round here. Some of them go out to work, you know, while their children are at school. Now they will have to stop work to look after them."

The news buzzed round Greenglades Wood like wildfire, and before long Rosemary and Amelia Rabbit had heard all about Ringo's training course.

"I have had an idea, sister," said Amelia, as they sat making crochet mittens beside the fire that evening. "We could start a playgroup for the children while Mr Fox is away."

"What a splendid idea!" cried Rosemary. "We love children so much, it would be such fun. We will put a notice about it in Amanda Mole's shop first thing in the morning."

All the woodland mothers were delighted about the rabbits' idea, and on the following Monday all the school children arrived on Rosemary and Amelia's doorstep.

"Come in, dears!" said Amelia, opening the door. At this, the children at the back started pushing, and the ones at the front were shoved inside, yelling and crying and making an awful noise. Poor Amelia had not expected that!

Rosemary tried to calm them all down by bringing out a tray of walnut biscuits and milk, but the milk was spilt all over the carpet and there were crumbs everywhere.

"Oh dear, oh dear!" gasped Rosemary, waving her hands in the air.

"Sit down, everyone!" quavered Amelia, but nobody took any notice. They were making so much noise, fighting and chasing each other around, that they simply did not hear.

Henry, the biggest baby hedgehog, slipped outside while nobody was looking, and ran as fast as he could through Greenglades Wood to the tree where Wise Owl lived.

"Hello, young Henry!" said Pippin the squirrel, who was passing by. "What are you doing here at this time?"

"Oh Pippin, please help!" said Henry. "Please hop up that tree and wake Wise Owl for me."

Pippin looked horrified.

"Wake Wise Owl from his morning sleep?" he gasped. "He'll be furious!"

"Oh, please, Pippin," said Henry. "I can't climb up there myself, and it's very important."

"It had better be!" said Pippin, as he hurried up the tree and knocked on Wise Owl's front door.

Wise Owl was cross at first, but when he heard what Henry had to say he began to look very pleased indeed.

"It's not that the rabbits mean any harm," said Henry. "They are doing their best, but we all need a proper school, with a proper teacher. Like you, sir," he added.

Wise Owl's feathers fluffed out with pleasure.

"I'll come at once," he said to Henry. "Lead the way!"

Rosemary and Amelia Rabbit were very relieved to see Wise Owl coming to their rescue. They watched their charges marching back to school in a straight, orderly line, with Wise Owl swooping over them to make sure no one dawdled.

"It's not that I don't like children . . ." said Amelia.

"Of course not, dear," agreed Rosemary, sinking into a chair with a sigh and wiping her brow with a silk handkerchief.

Wise Owl soon had all the children sitting quietly at their school desks. He had a lovely time giving out orders, and strutting up and down. The children found his lessons very interesting, and they were sorry when Ringo Fox came back.

Ringo was too wily to allow Wise Owl to leave the school entirely. After a long talk over a glass of rosehip wine in Ringo's study, it was decided that Wise Owl would continue to teach the children in the afternoons while Ringo went jogging to keep fit. That solution made everyone happy – but it made Wise Owl the happiest of all!

The Intruder

Mr Badger was walking home one morning after a successful night's hunting when he heard an angry squawking ahead of him on the path.

"Whoever can be making that dreadful noise?" said Mr Badger to himself. As he turned the bend in the path he came upon an awful sight. A large kitten crouched there, but it was not the kitten making the noise. It was Charlie Crow – for he was being pinned to the ground by the kitten's paws!

"Here, stop that!" snapped Mr Badger, and the kitten was so surprised that it lifted its paw. Charlie flew at once to the safety of a high branch.

"Hooligan!" he squawked. "Can't a chap take a walk in peace? You could have done me some serious damage!"

"I don't know where you come from, young lad, but don't you know your woodland manners?" said Mr Badger sternly, glaring at the kitten and shaking his paw.

"No, what are they?" asked the kitten. "I'm from the farm, myself. I've just left home to make my way in the world," he added proudly.

"Well, you won't get far if you carry on like this," said Mr Badger. "I have several nephews in the Greenglades police force who would lock you up for attacking poor Charlie like that."

"It's natural, isn't it?" asked the kitten. "Cats catch birds – everyone knows that."

"Dear me, you have got a lot to learn, haven't you?" said Mr Badger, shaking his head. "There's a time and a place for everything, you know. You had better come along home with me and have a bite of breakfast. Then I can tell you a few things about life in this wood."

Amanda Mole was just opening up her shop when she saw Mr Badger enter his sett with the kitten.

"I must be seeing things," she thought, taking off her spectacles and wiping them on her apron. "Surely Mr Badger would never make friends with a creature like that!"

Nobody misses anything in Greenglades Wood, and lots of other animals had seen Mr Badger with the kitten. Those who had not seen them, heard about it all from Charlie Crow, who had nothing hurt but his pride.

"Fancy Mr Badger taking up with such a creature!" said Amelia Rabbit.

"I'd like a new padlock for our door, please, Amanda," said Rosemary. "You can't be too careful with ruffians like that about."

"There's no need to be scared, I'm sure," said Henrietta, trying to calm her friends. "I used to see his mother around the farm. She is quite a friendly young cat called Elsie, with ginger stripes just like this young lad." The rabbits closed their eyes and shuddered.

"Well, we're not taking any chances. We're going home now and staying there," they said, and scuttled away.

Alfie Fieldmouse and his family were even more terrified at the news that there was a cat living in the wood. They refused to leave their home at all just in case they saw it.

"Dear, oh dear!" said Amanda Mole when she heard this from Pippin. "The mice have always been so good at carrying messages for me. Now I'll have no one to run errands! It simply is not good enough. The kitten must be sent home. I shall have a firm word with Mr Badger."

She shut up the shop and marched in a determined sort of way to Mr Badger's front door. She gave three loud bangs on it, before she could get frightened and run away.

Mr Badger was surprised to see her, but he asked her in and invited her to sit in one of his large armchairs. Amanda did so, but not for one moment did she take her eyes off the chair opposite her own where the ginger kitten was curled up, peering at her out of one half-closed eye.

"Now, Ginger," said Mr Badger sternly. "Remember your woodland manners. Sit up and say good afternoon nicely to Mrs Mole. I only taught you this morning."

"Good afternoon nicely," said the kitten, stretching out a sleepy paw so that Amanda backed away in alarm.

"Good afternoon," replied Amanda, doing her best to be brave. "I've come to see how long you expect to be staying here."

"Don't know," said the kitten, and went back to sleep.

"I'm training him, you see," said Mr Badger, excitedly. "I'm teaching him the proper way to behave. He must learn not to pounce on other animals for no reason, and all that. I'm having lots of fun."

"Maybe you are," said Amanda, "but some of the rest of us are not. There are animals who are terrified to go outside their own front doors! It's not natural. Cats don't belong in woods."

"Well, Ginger seems to like it," said Mr Badger.

Amanda went back to her shop wondering what else she could do to make Mr Badger see what trouble his guest was causing. She felt so unhappy about things that instead of bustling about in her shop she sat down and poured herself a large cup of her favourite nettle tea.

She had just started to drink it when she had a horrible shock. The door opened – and in came the ginger kitten!

"Have you got any tinned pilchards?" he asked.

"N . . . no," said Amanda.

"Well, any sardines, then?"

"What are they?" asked Amanda.

The kitten sighed.

"I suppose it would be too much to ask if you've got a nice little piece of herring, or a kipper, wouldn't it?"

"Oh, I don't stock anything like that," said Amanda. "There isn't the call for it round here."

"What a place this is!" grumbled the kitten. "You can't go hunting when you feel like it, and you can't buy a tasty piece of fish in the shops. This is no fun. I'm going home."

Amanda watched through the window as Ginger made his way out of the shop and along the woodland path, not stopping even for a glance as he passed Mr Badger's door.

Much later, Mr Badger came into the shop looking worried. "Excuse me for butting in," he said to Henrietta Hedgehog, who was buying a jar of pickled hazelnuts. "Have you seen that kitten anywhere? He seems to have gone missing."

"Oh, yes!" Amanda said, smiling. "I couldn't sell him any fish, so he's gone back to the farm."

"The ingratitude of it!" said Mr Badger. "After all I did for him! What does he want fish for when he's got everything in my larder to choose from? It just shows you, it doesn't pay to do anyone a good turn!"

Henrietta watched him go and then turned to pat Amanda's hand.

"He'll get over it," she said. "And a lot of people will be glad the kitten has gone." She picked up the jar of pickled hazelnuts from the counter.

"But you know, he had his good points, that young cat. He taught my babies to keep themselves clean just like he does – and I'm very grateful to him for it!"

Christmas Comes Early

Amanda Mole had had a very busy morning. There had been more customers than usual in her shop, and a family of stoat children had knocked over a large display of bottles which had rolled everywhere. On top of that, Hugh Toad, the travelling salesman, had spent a lot of time trying to make her stock goods she did not want. Amanda was not in a very good mood.

Henrietta and Pippin, who came into the shop at the same time, spotted this at once. When Pippin picked up a large box on the counter and pulled out lots of dazzling long things made of paper, Amanda told him not to meddle in what was not his.

"I only wanted to see them," said Pippin.

"What are they?" asked Henrietta. "I have never seen anything like that before."

"Don't be silly," snapped Amanda. "Anyone can see that they are Christmas decorations."

Henrietta looked at Amanda in a puzzled sort of way, but she did not like to ask what Christmas decorations were as Amanda was obviously not in a chatty mood.

"That Hugh Toad, the salesman, left them this morning," said Amanda. "I tried to tell him that I didn't need them yet, but he went off without them. Now I've got to find somewhere to store them until the right time." She snatched up the box and disappeared into the back room with it.

"I . . . er . . . I think I'll come back later," said Pippin, "when she's feeling better."

"So will I," said Henrietta, and they both hurried away.

They walked along the path, chatting about this and that.
Henrietta was going to ask Pippin what Christmas
decorations were when Pippin saw a friend waving at him.

"Why, if it isn't Sam Squirrel," he said. "I haven't seen him
for ages. I must go and catch up on all his news. Cheerio,
Henrietta," and off he ran down the path.

Henrietta walked on, still wondering about the Christmas decorations, when she suddenly realised how long she had been chatting to Pippin and how late she was. She bustled back home as quickly as she could, all thoughts of Christmas banished from her head.

Meanwhile Amanda was having lunch. She was feeling a little guilty that she had been so snappy with Pippin and Henrietta. After all, it was not their fault that everything had gone wrong that morning. As she was sipping her nettle tea she remembered the puzzled look Henrietta had given her when she had mentioned Christmas. It occurred to her that Henrietta was fast asleep in the middle of winter and always missed the fun they had at Christmas.

"How silly of me," she said out loud. "Fancy me not thinking of that!" Then her little eyes twinkled behind her spectacles and she chuckled.

"What a splendid idea," she muttered to herself. "Yes, that's what I'll do."

That evening, with the greatest secrecy, Amanda called the woodland folk to her house to tell them her plan. They all huddled together in Amanda's back kitchen as she explained that Henrietta and her family were always tucked up fast asleep in their beds at Christmas time.

"My plan," Amanda whispered, "is to arrange a special Christmas party for them."

"But we can't do that if she and her babies are all asleep," said Wise Owl.

"Oh no," replied Amanda. "I mean have a Christmas party now so they don't miss all the fun!"

"What a splendid idea," cried Pippin. "I did not know you were so clever, Amanda. That will suit Mr Badger and I better too. We only enjoy Christmas if the weather is warm and we wake up from one of our long winter snoozes."

"We could hold the party at our house if you like," added Rosemary. "If we decorate Amanda's home Henrietta is sure to suspect something."

It was all agreed, and the animals scurried back to their homes feeling very excited about their secret plan.

A few days later Henrietta called on Rosemary and Amelia to see if they would watch out for her babies as she had to go out before they were due home from school. She knocked, called, "Coo-eee! It's only me – Henrietta," and went to pop her head round the door as she usually did. This time, though, she heard a shriek, followed by a gasp, and Rosemary cried,

"Oh, don't come in! Please wait!"

Henrietta heard a scuffle, and a pause, and finally Amelia opened the door a crack.

"What is it?" she said.

"You're terribly out of breath," said Henrietta. "Are you all right?"

"Perfectly," said Amelia. "Do you want us to see to the children? All right then. Goodbye," and she shut the door again, right in Henrietta's face.

Henrietta was telling Pippin about this later on.

"They have been acting very strangely," said Henrietta. "I was in Amanda Mole's shop yesterday and it looked as if Rosemary Rabbit had fallen over. She was crouching down beside the counter, over a large box which I could just see poking out from under her apron."

"Very odd," said Pippin, trying not to smile. "Whatever can be the matter?"

"I think they may be unwell," went on Henrietta, "so I am going to make a woolly shawl for each of them to make them feel better."

"What a good idea," said Pippin, relieved that Henrietta did not suspect the real reason for their behaviour.

The next day Pippin called on Henrietta to find her wrapping up the two shawls in pretty paper – blue for Amelia and pink for Rosemary. The five baby hedgehogs were dancing about the room with excitement at the thought of giving the rabbits a lovely surprise.

When the presents were ready, they all set off to the rabbits' burrow, talking as they walked along. When they stopped at the door Pippin gave a very loud cough.

"Oh dear, Pippin," said Henrietta, a little worried. "I do hope you are not ill too."

"Oh no," said Pippin, knocking at the door. "I'm fine."

Amelia opened the door and smiled at Pippin.

"Your signal was right on time," she grinned. "Come in, all of you."

As they went in the hedgehogs got a tremendous surpise!

All their friends were there. Rosemary stood near the door
to meet them, and behind her were Amanda, Alfie Fieldmouse
and his family, Charlie Crow, Wise Owl, Ringo Fox and even
Mr Badger! Behind them was a big fir tree all decorated with
glow-worms, tinsel and pretty stars and bells.

"It must be a Christmas tree!" cried the baby hedgehogs
gleefully.

"Yes," said the Wise Owl, "and this is a Christmas party! It's
an early one so that you can enjoy the fun before you snuggle
up in your beds for your winter sleep!"

"How lovely!" said Henrietta. They ate Christmas cake, made from Amanda's own recipe with lots of dried beetles in it, which was delicious. They played games, and pulled crackers, and everyone had a funny hat to wear. There were apples and nuts, and presents for everyone.

"What a good thing I brought these presents for our two hostesses," thought Henrietta as they played ring-a-ring-a-roses around the settee.

At last it was time for everyone to go home. It was very late. As they stepped out into the night, the baby hedgehogs squealed with delight, for the wood was cloaked in a heavy frost and everything glistened with a white glow.

"It's just like a real white Christmas!" said Charlie Crow.

"And that means it is time for us to go to sleep for the winter," said Henrietta. "Thank you, everyone, for such a lovely party. We have had a marvellous time."

Then she hurried the little hedgehogs into their beds, and
they all settled down for a long sleep, dreaming of Christmas
cake, and stars, and paper hats.